In praise of loving fathers, especially Curtis,
Steven, Joe, and Unk John
K. B.

First edition 2010

Library of Congress Cataloging-in-Publication Data

Bennett, Kelly.
Dad and Pop / Kelly Bennett ; illustrated by Paul Meisel. — 1st ed.
p. cm.
Summary: A little girl celebrates her two fathers, who are very different
except in one very important way.
ISBN 978-0-7636-3379-0
[1. Fathers—Fiction.] I. Meisel, Paul, ill. II. Title.
PZ7.B4425Dad 2010
[E]—dc22   2009021486

10 11 12 13 14 15 CCP 10 9 8 7 6 5 4 3 2 1

Printed in Shenzhen, Guangdong, China

This book was typeset in Malonia Voigo.
The illustrations were done in watercolor, acrylic, and pastel.

Candlewick Press
99 Dover Street
Somerville, Massachusetts 02144

visit us at www.candlewick.com

AN ODE to FATHERS & STEPFATHERS

Dad and Pop

Kelly Bennett

illustrated by Paul Meisel

CANDLEWICK PRESS

I have two fathers.

I call this one Dad,

and this one Pop.

To meet them, you'd think Dad and Pop
were as different as two fathers could be.

Pop is bald.

Dad is not.

Dad is tall.

Pop is not.

Pop wears boots.

Dad wears suits.

Pop takes
pictures.

Dad takes naps.

Dad's into gadgets.

Pop's into plants.

Dad likes to fish.

Pop *is* a fish.

Dad and I
play sports.

Pop and I
play games.

Pop and I swap stories.

Dad and I swap jokes.

Dad teaches me to cook.

So does Pop.

Pop teaches me to paint.

So does Dad.

Dad loves music.

So does Pop.

Pop loves biking.

So does Dad.

They both help me.

They both cheer me.

In some ways Dad and Pop
are as different as can be.
But in the most important way
they are exactly the same—

They both

Dad and me.

MUSEUM
ADMIT ONE
ADMIT ONE

GLUE STICK

love me!

SEEDS

Pop and me.

31901047130366